P9-DCP-604

CLASSICS ILLUSTRATED™

presents

HAMLET

by William Shakespeare

CLASSICS ILLUSTRATED: HAMLET
ISBN: 9781910619704

Published by CCS Books
A trading name of Classic Comic Store Ltd.
Unit B, Castle Industrial Park, Pear Tree Lane, Newbury, Berkshire, RG14 2EZ, UK

Email: enquiries@ccsbooks.com
Tel: UK 01635 30890

First CCS Books edition: January 2016

Painted cover: Alex A. Blum
Illustrated by: Alex A. Blum
Adaptation: Samuel Willinsky
Re-origination: Bruce Downey
New cover design: Ray Lipscombe
Additional material: Debra Doyle

Printed in China

HAMLET
By WILLIAM SHAKESPEARE
HAMLET WAS CALLED HOME TO DENMARK FROM GERMANY BY THE SUDDEN DEATH OF HIS FATHER, THE KING. ON HIS RETURN TO THE ROYAL CASTLE AT ELSINORE, HAMLET WAS SHOCKED TO FIND THAT HIS MOTHER HAD WAITED ONLY A FEW WEEKS AFTER HER HUSBAND'S DEATH BEFORE MARRYING AGAIN... THIS TIME TO CLAUDIUS, THE LATE KING'S BROTHER. BY THIS MARRIAGE, CLAUDIUS WAS ABLE TO SEIZE THE THRONE WHICH RIGHTFULLY BELONGED TO HAMLET. HAMLET WAS DEEPLY GRIEVED BY HIS FATHER'S DEATH AND EQUALLY BITTER OVER HIS MOTHER'S HASTY REMARRIAGE.
NOW, ON WITH THE PLAY...
ILLUSTRATED BY ALEX A. BLUM

IT IS MIDNIGHT AND THE CASTLE GUARD IS CHANGING...
STAND AND UNFOLD YOURSELF.
LONG LIVE THE KING.
BERNARDO?
HE. 'TIS NOW STRUCK TWELVE: GET THEE TO BED, FRANCISCO.
FOR THIS RELIEF MUCH THANKS; 'TIS BITTER COLD.
IF YOU DO MEET HORATIO AND MARCELLUS, THE RIVALS* OF MY WATCH, BID THEM MAKE HASTE.
*PARTNERS
I THINK I HEAR THEM. STAND, HO! WHO IS THERE?
FRIENDS TO THIS GROUND.
AND LIEGEMAN TO THE DANE.
GIVE YOU GOOD-NIGHT.
FAREWELL, HONEST SOLDIER.

WELCOME, HORATIO; WELCOME, GOOD MARCELLUS.
HAS THIS THING APPEAR'D AGAIN TO-NIGHT?
I HAVE SEEN NOTHING.
HORATIO SAYS 'TIS BUT OUR FANTASY, AND WILL NOT LET BELIEF TAKE HOLD OF HIM TOUCHING THIS DREADED SIGHT, TWICE SEEN BY US; THEREFORE, I HAVE ENTREATED HIM ALONG WITH US TO WATCH THE MINUTES OF THIS NIGHT, THAT IF AGAIN THIS APPARITION COME, HE MAY APPROVE* OUR EYES AND SPEAK TO IT.
*CONFIRM
WELL, SIT WE DOWN, AND LET US HEAR BERNARDO SPEAK OF THIS.
LAST NIGHT, WHEN YOND SAME STAR THAT'S WESTWARD FROM THE POLE HAD MADE HIS COURSE T'ILLUME THAT PART OF HEAVEN WHERE NOW IT BEAMS, MARCELLUS AND MYSELF, THE BELL THEN BEATING ONE...
PEACE, BREAK THEE OFF! LOOK WHERE IT COMES AGAIN!
IN THE SAME FIGURE, LIKE THE KING THAT'S DEAD!

THOU ART A SCHOLAR; SPEAK TO IT, HORATIO
LOOKS IT NOT LIKE THE KING? MARK* IT, HORATIO.
MOST LIKE; IT HARROWS ME WITH FEAR AND WONDER.
*NOTE
IT WOULD BE SPOKE TO.
QUESTION IT, HORATIO.
WHAT ART THOUGH THAT USURP'ST THIS TIME OF NIGHT, TOGETHER WITH THAT FAIR AND WARLIKE FORM IN WHICH THE MAJESTY OF BURIED DENMARK DID SOMETIMES MARCH? I CHARGE THEE, SPEAK.
IT IS OFFENDED.
SEE, IT STALKS AWAY!
STAY! SPEAK, SPEAK!

HOW NOW, HORATIO? YOU TREMBLE AND LOOK PALE; IS NOT THIS SOMETHING MORE THAN FANTASY?
BEFORE MY GOD, I MIGHT NOT BELIEVE WITHOUT THE SENSIBLE AND TRUE AVOUCH* OF MINE OWN EYES.
'TIS GONE AND WILL NOT ANSWER.
*PROOF
BUT SOFT, BEHOLD! LO, IT COMES AGAIN! I'LL CROSS IT, THOUGH IT BLAST ME.
STAY, ILLUSION! IF THOU HAST ANY SOUND, OR USE OF VOICE, SPEAK TO ME; STAY, AND SPEAK!
THE GHOST IS ABOUT TO SPEAK WHEN, SUDDENLY, A COCK CROWS IN THE DISTANCE, ANNOUNCING THE BREAK OF DAY. THE GHOST ABRUPTLY TURNS AND STARTS TO LEAVE...
STOP IT, MARCELLUS!
SHALL I STRIKE AT IT?
DO, IF IT WILL NOT STAND.
'TIS HERE!
'TIS HERE!

'TIS GONE! WE DO IT WRONG TO OFFER IT THE SHOW OF VIOLENCE; FOR IT IS, AS THE AIR, INVULNERABLE, AND OUR VAIN BLOWS MALICIOUS MOCKERY.
IT WAS ABOUT TO SPEAK, WHEN THE COCK CREW.
BREAK WE OUR WATCH UP; AND LET US IMPART WHAT WE HAVE SEEN UNTO YOUNG HAMLET; FOR, UPON MY LIFE, THIS SPIRIT, DUMB TO US, WILL SPEAK TO HIM.
LET'S DO'T, I PRAY; AND I KNOW WHERE WE SHALL FIND HIM.

INSIDE THE ROYAL CASTLE, HAMLET SITS ALONE, GIVING VOICE TO HIS GRIEF AND BITTERNESS...
O, THAT THIS TOO TOO SOLID FLESH WOULD MELT,
THAW AND RESOLVE ITSELF INTO A DEW!
OR THAT THE EVERLASTING HAD NOT FIX'D
HIS CANON 'GAINST SELF-SLAUGHTER! O GOD! GOD!
HOW WEARY, STALE, FLAT AND UNPROFITABLE
SEEM TO ME ALL THE USES OF THIS WORLD!
FIE ON'T! AH FIE! 'TIS AN UNWEEDED GARDEN
THAT GROWS TO SEED; THINGS RANK AND GROSS IN NATURE
POSSESS IT MERELY. THAT IT SHOULD COME TO THIS!
BUT TWO MONTHS DEAD! NAY, NOT SO MUCH, NOT TWO:
SO EXCELLENT A KING; THAT WAS, TO THIS,
HYPERION TO A SATYR: SO LOVING TO MY MOTHER,
THAT HE MIGHT NOT BETEEM THE WINDS OF HEAVEN
VISIT HER FACE TOO ROUGHLY. HEAVEN AND EARTH!
MUST I REMEMBER? WHY, SHE WOULD HANG ON HIM,
AS IF INCREASE OF APPETITE HAD GROWN
BY WHAT IT FED ON: AND YET, WITHIN A MONTH -
LET ME NOT THINK ON'T. - FRAILTY, THY NAME IS WOMAN!
A LITTLE MONTH, OR ERE THOSE SHOES WERE OLD
WITH WHICH SHE FOLLOWED MY POOR FATHER'S BODY,
LIKE NIOBE, ALL TEARS: - WHY SHE, EVEN SHE, -
O GOD! A BEAST THAT WANTS DISCOURSE OF REASON
WOULD HAVE MOURN'D LONGER, - MARRIED WITH MY UNCLE,
MY FATHER'S BROTHER, BUT NO MORE LIKE MY FATHER
THAN I TO HERCULES: WITHIN A MONTH;
ERE YET THE SALT OF MOST UNRIGHTEOUS TEARS
HAD LEFT THE FLUSHING IN HER GALLED EYES,
SHE MARRIED. IT IS NOT, NOR IT CANNOT COME TO GOOD:
BUT BREAK MY HEART, FOR I MUST HOLD MY TONGUE!
A MOMENT LATER, HORATIO, MARCELLUS AND BERNARDO ENTER AND TELL HAMLET ALL THAT HAD HAPPENED THE NIGHT BEFORE...
I WILL WATCH TONIGHT; PERCHANCE 'T WILL WALK AGAIN.
MY FATHER'S SPIRIT IN ARMS. ALL IS NOT WELL; I DOUBT SOME FOUL PLAY; WOULD THE NIGHT WERE COME. TILL THEN SIT STILL, MY SOUL: FOUL DEEDS WILL RISE, THOUGH ALL THE EARTH O'ERWHELM THEM TO MEN'S EYES.
MEANWHILE, LAERTES, SON OF THE KING'S CHIEF ADVISOR, POLONIUS, READIES HIMSELF TO TRAVEL TO FRANCE. BEFORE GOING, HE WARNS HIS SISTER, OPHELIA, NOT TO RETURN HAMLET'S LOVE FOR HER. POLONIUS ENTERS AND CAUTIONS HIS SON AS TO HIS BEHAVIOUR WHILE IN FRANCE...
GIVE THY THOUGHTS NO TONGUE, NOR ANY UNPROPORTION'D THOUGHT HIS ACT;
...THIS ABOVE ALL: TO THINE OWN SELF BE TRUE, AND IT MUST FOLLOW, AS THE NIGHT THE DAY, THOU CANST NOT BE FALSE TO ANY MAN. FAREWELL; MY BLESSING SEASON THIS IN THEE.
AFTER LAERTES LEAVES, POLONIUS ALSO WARNS OPHELIA AGAINST RETURNING HAMLET'S LOVE...
DO NOT BELIEVE HIS VOWS; I WOULD NOT, IN PLAIN TERMS, FROM THIS TIME FORTH HAVE YOU GIVE TALK WITH THE LORD HAMLET.

THAT NIGHT, ACCOMPANIED BY HORATIO AND MARCELLUS, HAMLET GOES TO MEET THE GHOST. EXACTLY AT MIDNIGHT, THE GHOST APPEARS...
ANGELS AND MINISTERS OF GRACE DEFEND US! BE THOU A SPIRIT OF HEALTH OR GOBLIN DAMN'D, BRING WITH THEE AIRS FROM HEAVEN OR BLASTS FROM HELL, BE THY INTENTS WICKED OR CHARITABLE, THOU COM'ST IN SUCH A QUESTIONABLE SHAPE THAT I WILL SPEAK TO THEE. I'LL CALL THEE HAMLET, KING, FATHER, ROYAL DANE - O, ANSWER ME! WHAT MAY THIS MEAN, THAT THOU, DEAD CORSE,* AGAIN IN COMPLETE STEEL REVISITS THUS?
*CORPSE

THE GHOST BECKONS HAMLET TO FOLLOW IT...
YOU SHALL NOT GO, MY LORD.
HOLD OFF YOUR HANDS. GO ON, I'LL FOLLOW THEE.
HAMLET FOLLOWS THE GHOST DOWN THE STAIRWAY TO A DESERTED SPOT. THE GHOST THEN TURNS AND SPEAKS...
I AM THY FATHER'S SPIRIT - DOOMED TO WALK THE NIGHT, AND FOR THE DAY CONFIN'D TO FAST IN FIRES, TILL THE FOUL CRIMES DONE IN MY DAYS OF NATURE ARE PURGED AWAY. LIST! IF THOU DIDST EVER THY DEAR FATHER LOVE, REVENGE HIS FOUL AND MOST UNNATURAL MURDER.
MURDER! HASTE ME TO KNOW'T, THAT I MAY SWEEP TO MY REVENGE.
'TIS GIVEN OUT THAT, SLEEPING IN MY ORCHARD, A SERPENT STUNG ME; BUT KNOW, THE SERPENT THAT DID STING THY FATHER'S LIFE NOW WEARS HIS CROWN.
"SLEEPING WITHIN MINE ORCHARD, UPON MY SECURE HOUR, THY UNCLE STOLE WITH JUICE OF CURSED HEBONA* IN A VIAL..."
*A POISONOUS WEED

"AND IN MINE EARS DID POUR THIS LEP'ROUS DISTILMENT; WHOSE EFFECT HOLDS SUCH AN ENMITY WITH BLOOD OF MAN THAT SWIFT AS QUICKSILVER IT COURSES THROUGH THE NATURAL GATES AND ALLEYS OF THE BODY."
"THUS WAS I, SLEEPING, BY A BROTHER'S HAND OF LIFE, OF CROWN, OF QUEEN, AT ONCE DISPATCH'D..."
O, HORRIBLE! MOST HORRIBLE! IF THOU HAST NATURE IN THEE, BEAR IT NOT. BUT, HOWSOEVER THOU PURSUEST THIS ACT, TAINT NOT THY MIND, NOR LET THY SOUL CONTRIVE AGAINST THY MOTHER AUGHT; LEAVE HER TO HEAVEN.
AS THEY SPEAK, A COCK CROWS AND DAWN BREAKS. THE GHOST MUST LEAVE...
FARE THEE WELL AT ONCE! ADIEU, ADIEU! REMEMBER ME!
AFTER THE GHOST HAS GONE, HORATIO AND MARCELLUS ASK TO BE INFORMED AS TO WHAT THE GHOST HAD SAID. INSTEAD, HAMLET SWEARS THEM TO SECRECY...
NEVER MAKE KNOWN WHAT YOU HAVE SEEN TO-NIGHT. SWEAR IT.
WE WILL NOT, WE SWEAR IT.

AS DAYS PASS, A STRANGE MADNESS, PART REAL AND PART FEIGNED, COMES OVER HAMLET. ONE DAY, HE ENTER OPHELIA'S ROOM AND SHOCKS HER BY HIS STRANGE BEHAVIOUR. SHE REPORTS THIS TO HER FATHER...
"AS I WAS SEWING, LORD HAMLET, NO HAT UPON HIS HEAD, HIS STOCKINGS FOULED, PALE AS HIS SHIRT, AND WITH A LOOK SO PITEOUS IN PURPORT* COMES BEFORE ME..."
*EXPRESSION
MAD FOR THY LOVE?
MY LORD, I DO NOT KNOW; BUT TRULY, I DO FEAR IT.
WHAT SAID HE?
HE TOOK ME BY THE WRIST AND HELD ME HARD; THEN GOES HE TO THE LENGTH OF ALL HIS ARM, AND, WITH HIS OTHER HAND O'ER HIS BROW, HE FALLS TO PERUSAL OF MY FACE. LONG STAY'D HE SO. THAT DONE, HE LETS ME GO; AND, WITH HIS HEAD OVER HIS SHOULDER TURN'D, HE SEEMED TO FIND HIS WAY WITHOUT HIS EYES, FOR OUT O'DOORS HE WENT WITHOUT THEIR HELP. AND, TO THE LAST, BENDED THEIR LIGHT ON ME.
THIS IS THE VERY ECSTASY* OF LOVE. HAVE YOU GIVEN HIM ANY HARD WORDS OF LATE?
NO, BUT AS YOU DID COMMAND, I DID REPEL HIS LETTERS AND DENIED HIS ACCESS TO ME.
*MADNESS
THAT HATH MADE HIM MAD. COME, WE GO TO THE KING. THIS MUST BE KNOWN.
MEANWHILE, KING CLAUDIUS AND QUEEN GERTRUDE, IN AN EFFORT TO DISCOVER THE CAUSE OF HAMLET'S STRANGE BEHAVIOUR, ORDER TWO OF HAMLET'S FRIENDS, ROSENCRANTZ AND GUILDENSTERN TO SPY ON HAMLET...
DRAW HIM ON TO PLEASURES AND GATHER SO MUCH AS FROM OCCASIONS YOU MAY GLEAN.
WE BOTH OBEY.

POLONIUS THEN ENTERS AND TELLS THE KING AND QUEEN OF HAMLET'S ACTIONS...
SINCE BREVITY IS THE SOUL OF WIT, I WILL BE BRIEF. YOUR NOBLE SON IS MAD: AND NOW REMAINS THAT WE FIND OUT THE CAUSE OF THIS EFFECT. I HAVE A DAUGHTER WHO, IN HER DUTY, HATH GIVEN ME THIS NOW GATHER AND SURMISE.
POLONIUS READS FROM A LETTER HAMLET HAD SENT OPHELIA...
"TO THE CELESTIAL AND MY SOUL'S IDOL, THE MOST BEAUTIFIED OPHELIA: DOUBT THOU THE STARS ARE FIRE, DOUBT THAT THE SUN DOTH MOVE, DOUBT TRUTH TO BE A LIAR, BUT NEVER DOUBT I LOVE."
THIS IN OBEDIENCE HATH MY DAUGHTER SHOWN ME. AND MY YOUNG MISTRESS THUS DID I BESPEAK: "LORD HAMLET IS A PRINCE OUT OF THY STAR. THIS MUST NOT BE." THEN I PRESCRIPTS* GAVE HER – THAT SHE LOCK HERSELF FROM HIS MESSENGERS, RECEIVE NO TOKENS. AND HE, REPELL'D, FELL INTO THE MADNESS WHEREIN NOW HE RAVES.
DO YOU THINK 'TIS THIS?
*ORDERS
HATH THERE BEEN SUCH A TIME THAT I HAVE POSITIVELY SAID, "'TIS SO," WHEN IT PROVED OTHERWISE?
HOW MAY WE TRY IT FURTHER?
SOMETIMES HE WALKS FOUR HOURS TOGETHER HERE IN THE LOBBY. AT SUCH A TIME, I'LL LOOSE MY DAUGHTER TO HIM: BE YOU AND I BEHIND THE ARRAS* THEN; MARK THE ENCOUNTER: IF HE LOVE HER NOT, AND BE NOT FROM HIS REASON FALL'N THEREON, LET ME BE NO ASSISTANT FOR A STATE.
WE WILL TRY IT.
*TAPESTRY

THE FOLLOWING DAY, POLONIUS SETS THE STAGE FOR HIS SCHEME. HAMLET, COMPLETELY UNAWARE OF THE PEOPLE ABOUT HIM, ENTERS. HE IS IN DEEP THOUGHT AND IS CONTEMPLATING SUICIDE...
TO BE, OR NOT TO BE: THAT IS THE QUESTION:
WHETHER 'TIS NOBLER IN THE MIND TO SUFFER
THE SLINGS AND ARROWS OF OUTRAGEOUS FORTUNE,
OR TO TAKE ARMS AGAINST A SEA OF TROUBLES,
AND BY OPPOSING END THEM. TO DIE, TO SLEEP--
NO MORE; AND BY A SLEEP TO SAY WE END
THE HEART-ACHE AND THE THOUSAND NATURAL SHOCKS
THAT FLESH IS HEIR TO; 'TIS A CONSUMMATION
DEVOUTLY TO BE WISH'D; TO DIE; TO SLEEP;
TO SLEEP, PERCHANCE TO DREAM; AYE, THERE'S THE RUB;
FOR IN THAT SLEEP OF DEATH WHAT DREAMS MAY COME,
WHEN WE HAVE SHUFFLED OFF THIS MORTAL COIL,
MUST GIVE US PAUSE; THERE'S THE RESPECT
THAT MAKES CALAMITY OF SO LONG LIFE:
FOR WHO WOULD BEAR THE WHIPS AND SCORNS OF TIME,
TH' OPPRESSORS'S WRONG, THE PROUD MAN'S CONTUMELY,
THE PANGS OF DISPRIZ'D[1] LOVE, THE LAW'S DELAY,
THE INSOLENCE OF OFFICE, AND THE SPURNS
THAT PATIENT MERIT OF TH' UNWORTHY TAKES,
WHEN HE HIMSELF MIGHT HIS QUIETUS MAKE
WITH A BARE BODKIN? WHO WOULD FARDELS[2] BEAR,
TO GRUNT AND SWEAT UNDER A WEARY LIFE,
BUT THAT THE DREAD OF SOMETHING AFTER DEATH,
THE UNDISCOVER'D COUNTRY FROM WHOSE BOURN
NO TRAVELLER RETURNS, PUZZLES THE WILL
AND MAKES US RATHER BEAR THOSE ILLS WE HAVE
THAN TO FLY TO OTHERS THAT WE KNOW NOT OF?
THUS CONSCIENCE[3] DOES MAKE COWARDS OF US ALL;
AND THUS THE NATIVE HUE OF RESOLUTION
IS SICKLIED O'ER WITH THE PALE CAST OF THOUGHT,
AND ENTERPRISES OF GREAT PITCH AND MOMENT
WITH THIS REGARD THEIR CURRENTS TURN AWRY,
AND LOSE THE NAME OF ACTION. -- SOFT YOU NOW,
THE FAIR OPHELIA! -- NYMPH, IN THY ORISONS[4]
BE ALL MY SINS REMEMBER'D.
[1]BELITTLED
[2]BURDENS
[3]SELF-EXAMINATION
[4]PRAYERS

AS HAMLET ENDS HIS SOLILOQUY, OPHELIA APPROACHES HIM...
MY LORD, I HAVE REMEMBRANCES OF YOURS THAT I HAVE LONGED LONG TO RE-DELIVER; I PRAY YOU NOW RECEIVE THEM.
NO, NOT I; I NEVER GAVE YOU AUGHT.
MY LORD, YOU KNOW RIGHT WELL YOU DID, AND, WITH THEM, WORDS OF SO SWEET BREATH COMPOS'D AS MADE THE THINGS MORE RICH.
I DID LOVE YOU ONCE.
INDEED, YOU MADE ME BELIEVE SO.
YOU SHOULD NOT HAVE BELIEVED ME. I LOVED YOU NOT.
I WAS THE MORE DECEIVED.
GET THEE TO A NUNNERY; WHY WOULDST THOU BE A BREEDER OF SINNERS? OR, IF THOU WILT NEEDS MARRY, MARRY A FOOL; FOR WISE MEN KNOW WELL ENOUGH WHAT MONSTERS YOU MAKE OF THEM. TO A NUNNERY, GO, AND QUICKLY, TOO. FAREWELL!
HEAVENLY POWERS, RESTORE HIM! O, WHAT A NOBLE MIND IS HERE O'ERTHROWN! O, WOE IS ME, T'HAVE SEEN WHAT I HAVE SEEN, SEE WHAT I SEE!
LOVE! HIS AFFECTIONS DO NOT THAT WAY TEND: THERE'S SOMETHING IN HIS SOUL OVER WHICH HIS MELANCHOLY SITS ON BROOD. TO PREVENT DANGER, I HAVE IN QUICK DETERMINATION THUS SET IT DOWN - HE SHALL WITH SPEED TO ENGLAND. HAPLY THE SEAS AND COUNTRIES DIFFERENT WITH VARIABLE OBJECTS SHALL EXPEL THIS MATTER IN HIS HEART.

THAT DAY, A GROUP OF ACTORS APPEARS AT THE CASTLE. HAMLET SPEAKS TO THE LEADER...
CAN YOU PLAY "THE MURDER OF GONZAGO?"
AYE, MY LORD.
WE'LL HA'T TO-MORROW NIGHT. YOU COULD STUDY A SPEECH OF SOME DOZEN OR SIXTEEN LINES WHICH I WOULD INSERT IN IT, COULD YOU NOT?
AYE, MY LORD. AND FOR NOW, FAREWELL.
I'LL HAVE THESE PLAYERS PLAY SOMETHING LIKE THE MURDER OF MY FATHER BEFORE MINE UNCLE. I'LL OBSERVE HIS LOOKS; IF HE BUT BLENCH* I KNOW MY COURSE. THE PLAY'S THE THING WHEREIN I'LL CATCH THE CONSCIENCE OF THE KING.
*TURN WHITE
THE FOLLOWING DAY, HAMLET SEEKS OUT HIS GOOD FRIEND, HORATIO, AND ASKS HIS ASSISTANCE...
THERE IS A PLAY TONIGHT BEFORE THE KING; ONE SCENE OF IT COMES NEAR THE CIRCUMSTANCE OF MY FATHER'S DEATH. OBSERVE MY UNCLE. GIVE HIM HEEDFUL NOTE. I MINE EYES WILL RIVET TO HIS FACE AND AFTER, WE WILL BOTH OUR JUDGEMENTS JOIN IN CENSURE OF HIS SEEMING.
THAT EVENING, ROSENCRANTZ AND GUILDENSTERN REPORT THEY CAN LEARN NOTHING OF HAMLET'S MADNESS. THEN THE KING AND QUEEN AND ALL THE ROYAL COURT GO TO ATTEND THE PLAY...

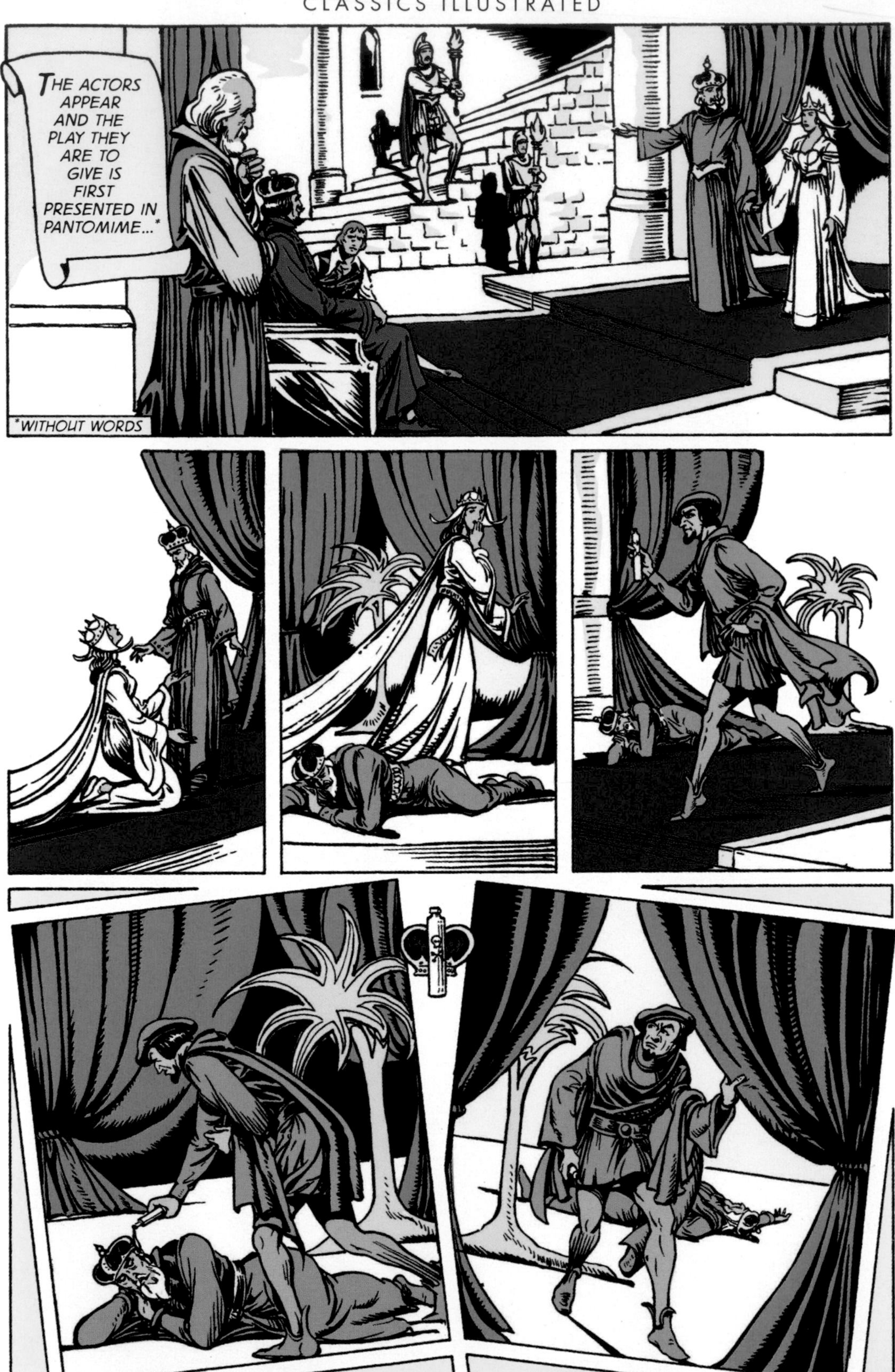
THE ACTORS APPEAR AND THE PLAY THEY ARE TO GIVE IS FIRST PRESENTED IN PANTOMIME...*
*WITHOUT WORDS

PUZZLED, OPHELIA TURNS TO HAMLET...
WHAT MEANS THIS, MY LORD? BELIKE THIS SHOW IMPORTS THE ARGUMENT OF THE PLAY?
WE SHALL KNOW BY THIS FELLOW.
FOR US AND FOR OUR TRAGEDY, HERE STOOPING TO YOUR CLEMENCY, WE BEG YOUR HEARING PATIENTLY.
THE SPEAKING PLAY BEGINS. IT IS A REPETITION OF THE PANTOMIME PLAY EXCEPT THAT THERE ARE NOW SPOKEN LINES. WHEN THE ACTORS ONCE AGAIN PLAY THE POISONING SCENE, KING CLAUDIUS SUDDENLY LEAPS TO HIS FEET AND SCREAMS...
GIVE ME LIGHT!

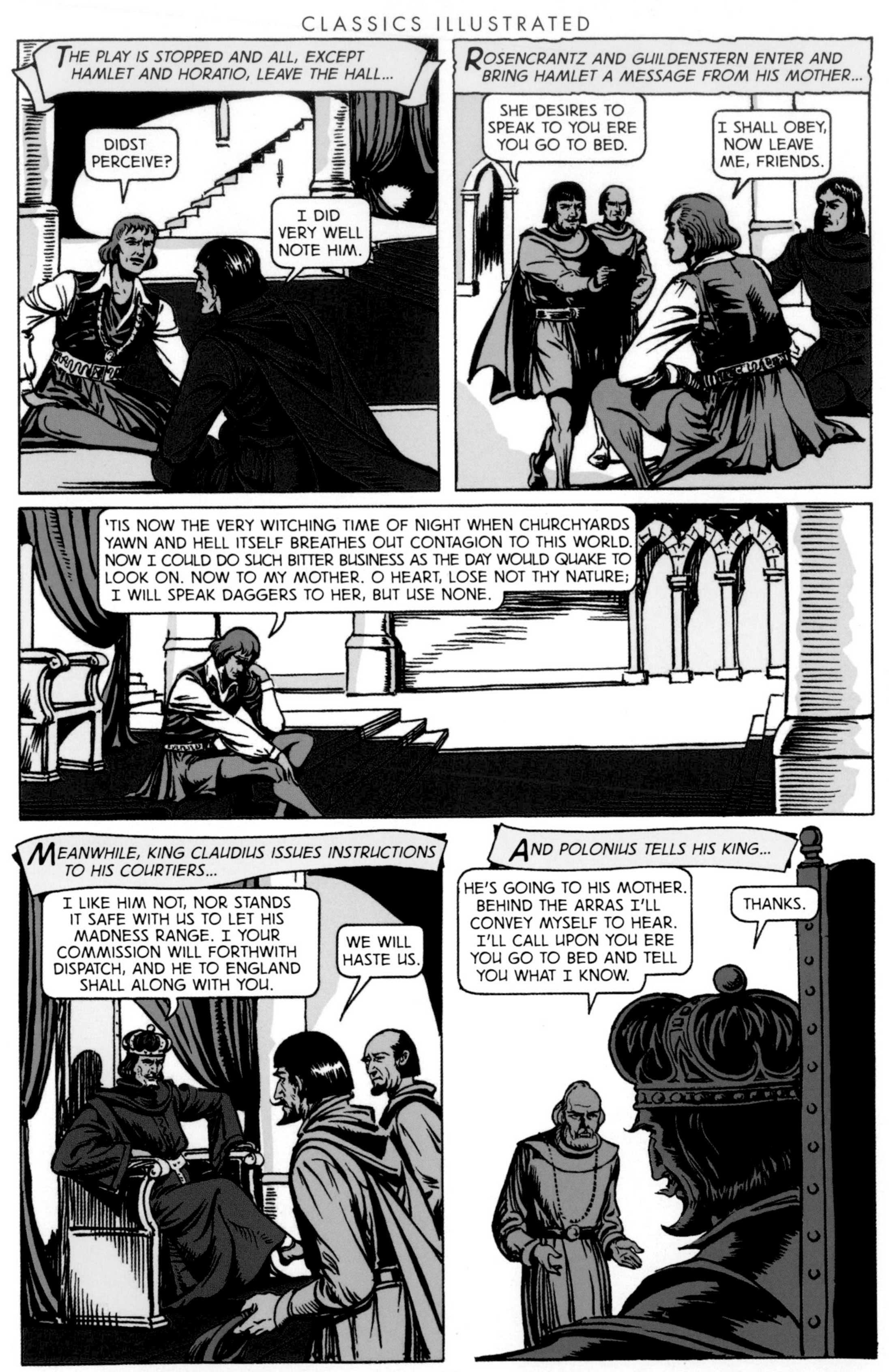
THE PLAY IS STOPPED AND ALL, EXCEPT HAMLET AND HORATIO, LEAVE THE HALL...
DIDST PERCEIVE?
I DID VERY WELL NOTE HIM.
ROSENCRANTZ AND GUILDENSTERN ENTER AND BRING HAMLET A MESSAGE FROM HIS MOTHER...
SHE DESIRES TO SPEAK TO YOU ERE YOU GO TO BED.
I SHALL OBEY, NOW LEAVE ME, FRIENDS.
'TIS NOW THE VERY WITCHING TIME OF NIGHT WHEN CHURCHYARDS YAWN AND HELL ITSELF BREATHES OUT CONTAGION TO THIS WORLD. NOW I COULD DO SUCH BITTER BUSINESS AS THE DAY WOULD QUAKE TO LOOK ON. NOW TO MY MOTHER. O HEART, LOSE NOT THY NATURE; I WILL SPEAK DAGGERS TO HER, BUT USE NONE.
MEANWHILE, KING CLAUDIUS ISSUES INSTRUCTIONS TO HIS COURTIERS...
I LIKE HIM NOT, NOR STANDS IT SAFE WITH US TO LET HIS MADNESS RANGE. I YOUR COMMISSION WILL FORTHWITH DISPATCH, AND HE TO ENGLAND SHALL ALONG WITH YOU.
WE WILL HASTE US.
AND POLONIUS TELLS HIS KING...
HE'S GOING TO HIS MOTHER. BEHIND THE ARRAS I'LL CONVEY MYSELF TO HEAR. I'LL CALL UPON YOU ERE YOU GO TO BED AND TELL YOU WHAT I KNOW.
THANKS.

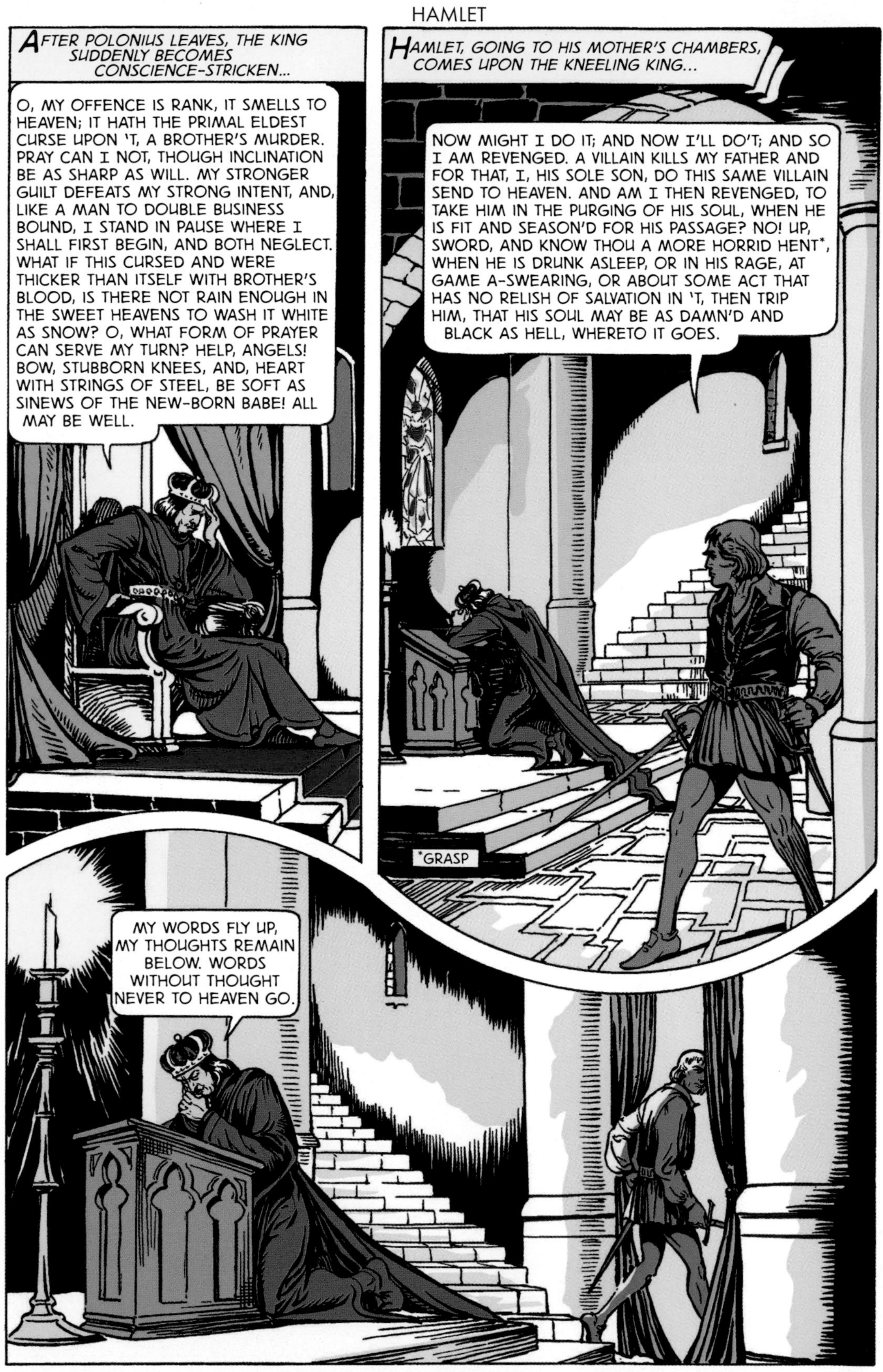
AFTER POLONIUS LEAVES, THE KING SUDDENLY BECOMES CONSCIENCE-STRICKEN...
O, MY OFFENCE IS RANK, IT SMELLS TO HEAVEN; IT HATH THE PRIMAL ELDEST CURSE UPON 'T, A BROTHER'S MURDER. PRAY CAN I NOT, THOUGH INCLINATION BE AS SHARP AS WILL. MY STRONGER GUILT DEFEATS MY STRONG INTENT, AND, LIKE A MAN TO DOUBLE BUSINESS BOUND, I STAND IN PAUSE WHERE I SHALL FIRST BEGIN, AND BOTH NEGLECT. WHAT IF THIS CURSED AND WERE THICKER THAN ITSELF WITH BROTHER'S BLOOD, IS THERE NOT RAIN ENOUGH IN THE SWEET HEAVENS TO WASH IT WHITE AS SNOW? O, WHAT FORM OF PRAYER CAN SERVE MY TURN? HELP, ANGELS! BOW, STUBBORN KNEES, AND, HEART WITH STRINGS OF STEEL, BE SOFT AS SINEWS OF THE NEW-BORN BABE! ALL MAY BE WELL.
HAMLET, GOING TO HIS MOTHER'S CHAMBERS, COMES UPON THE KNEELING KING...
NOW MIGHT I DO IT; AND NOW I'LL DO'T; AND SO I AM REVENGED. A VILLAIN KILLS MY FATHER AND FOR THAT, I, HIS SOLE SON, DO THIS SAME VILLAIN SEND TO HEAVEN. AND AM I THEN REVENGED, TO TAKE HIM IN THE PURGING OF HIS SOUL, WHEN HE IS FIT AND SEASON'D FOR HIS PASSAGE? NO! UP, SWORD, AND KNOW THOU A MORE HORRID HENT*, WHEN HE IS DRUNK ASLEEP, OR IN HIS RAGE, AT GAME A-SWEARING, OR ABOUT SOME ACT THAT HAS NO RELISH OF SALVATION IN 'T, THEN TRIP HIM, THAT HIS SOUL MAY BE AS DAMN'D AND BLACK AS HELL, WHERETO IT GOES.
*GRASP
MY WORDS FLY UP, MY THOUGHTS REMAIN BELOW. WORDS WITHOUT THOUGHT NEVER TO HEAVEN GO.

A SHORT WHILE LATER, HAMLET ENTERS HIS MOTHER'S CHAMBERS...
NOW, MOTHER, WHAT'S THE MATTER?
THOU HAST THY FATHER MUCH OFFENDED.
BEHIND THE ARRAS, POLONIUS STANDS LISTENING TO EVERY WORD.
MOTHER, YOU HAVE MY FATHER MUCH OFFENDED.
COME, COME, YOU ANSWER WITH AN IDLE TONGUE.
GO, GO, YOU QUESTION WITH A WICKED TONGUE.
HAVE YOU FORGOT ME?
NO, NOT SO; YOU ARE THE QUEEN, YOUR HUSBAND'S BROTHER'S WIFE; AND - WOULD IT WERE NOT SO! - YOU ARE MY MOTHER.
SIT YOU DOWN; YOU SHALL NOT BUDGE; YOU GO NOT TILL I SET YOU UP A GLASS* WHERE YOU MAY SEE THE INMOST PARTS OF YOU.
*MIRROR

WHAT WILT THOU DO? THOU WILT NOT MURDER ME? HELP, HO!
POLONIUS, THINKING THAT HAMLET IS MURDERING THE QUEEN, ALSO SHOUTS FOR HELP...
WHAT, HO! HELP!
HOW NOW! A RAT? DEAD!
O, I AM SLAIN!

O ME, WHAT HAST THOU DONE?
NAY, I KNOW NOT. IS IT THE KING?
O, WHAT A RASH AND BLOODY DEED IS THIS!
ALMOST AS BAD, GOOD MOTHER, AS KILL A KING, AND MARRY WITH HIS BROTHER.
AS KILL A KING?
AYE, LADY, 'TWAS MY WORD.
THOU WRETCHED, INTRUDING FOOL, FAREWELL! I TOOK THEE FOR THY BETTER.
LEAVE WRINGING OF YOUR HANDS; SIT DOWN AND LET ME WRING YOUR HEART; FOR SO I SHALL, IF IT BE MADE OF PENETRABLE STUFF.
WHAT HAVE I DONE, THAT THOU DAR'ST WAG THY TONGUE IN NOISE SO RUDE AGAINST ME?
SUCH AN ACT THAT BLURS THE GRACE AND BLUSH OF MODESTY, CALLS VIRTUE HYPOCRITE, TAKES OFF THE ROSE FROM THE FAIR FOREHEAD OF AN INNOCENT LOVE AND SETS A BLISTER THERE

LOOK HERE, UPON THIS PICTURE, AND ON THIS, THE COUNTERFEIT PRESENTMENT OF TWO BROTHERS. SEE WHAT A GRACE WAS SEATED ON THIS BROW: AN EYE LIKE MARS, TO THREATEN AND COMMAND, A STATION LIKE THE HERALD MERCURY NEW-LIGHTED ON A HEAVEN-KISSING HILL -- A COMBINATION AND A FORM INDEED, WHERE EVERY GOD DID SEEM TO SET HIS SEAL TO GIVE THE WORLD ASSURANCE OF A MAN: THIS WAS YOUR HUSBAND. LOOK YOU NOW WHAT FOLLOWS: HERE IS YOUR HUSBAND -- LIKE A MILDEW'D EAR, BLASTING HIS WHOLESOME BROTHER.
O HAMLET, SPEAK NO MORE: THOU TURN'ST MINE EYES INTO MY VERY SOUL, AND THERE I SEE SUCH BLACK AND GRAINED SPOTS AS WILL LEAVE THEIR TINCT.
BUT HAMLET'S ANGER MOUNTS WITH EVERY WORD AND HE CONTINUES AS THOUGH THE QUEEN HAD NOT SPOKEN...
A MURDERER AND A VILLAIN, A SLAVE THAT IS NOT TWENTIETH PART OF YOUR PRECEDENT LORD!
JUST THEN, THE GHOST ENTERS THE ROOM AND HAMLET BREAKS OFF HIS TIRADE. HE TURNS TO SPEAK TO THE SPECTRE OF HIS FATHER...
WHAT WOULD YOUR GRACIOUS FIGURE?
ALAS, HE'S MAD!

DO YOU NOT COME YOUR TARDY SON TO CHIDE, THAT, LAPSED IN TIME AND PASSION, LETS GO BY THE IMPORTANT ACTING OF YOUR DREAD COMMAND?

DO NOT FORGET! THIS VISITATION IS BUT TO WHET THY ALMOST BLUNTED PURPOSE. BUT, LOOK, AMAZEMENT ON THY MOTHER SITS; O, STEP BETWEEN HER AND HER FIGHTING SOUL. SPEAK TO HER, HAMLET.

THE QUEEN, OF COURSE, CANNOT SEE NOR HEAR THE GHOST...
HOW IS IT WITH YOU, LADY?
ALAS, HOW IS 'T WITH YOU, THAT YOU DO BEND YOUR EYE ON VACANCY? AND WITH THE AIR HOLD DISCOURSE? WHEREON DO YOU LOOK?
WHY, LOOK YOU THERE! LOOK HOW IT STEALS AWAY! MY FATHER, IN HIS HABIT AS HE LIVED! LOOK WHERE HE GOES, EVEN NOW, OUT AT THE PORTAL!
THIS IS THE VERY COINAGE OF YOUR BRAIN. O HAMLET, THOU HAS CLEFT MY HEART IN TWAIN.
THROW AWAY THE WORSER PART OF IT, AND LIVE THE PURER WITH THE OTHER HALF. I MUST TO ENGLAND; THERE'S LETTERS SEAL'D, AND MY TWO SCHOOL-FELLOWS, WHOM I WILL TRUST AS I WILL ADDERS* FANG'D, THEY BEAR THE MANDATE
*VERY POISONOUS SNAKES
THIS COUNSELLOR IS NOW MOST STILL. COME, SIR, TO DRAW TOWARD AN END WITH YOU. GOOD-NIGHT, MOTHER.
THE QUEEN TELLS THE KING OF THE EVENING'S EVENTS. THE KING, FEARFUL THAT HE MAY BE HAMLET'S NEXT VICTIM, AND TO HIDE THE FACT THAT HAMLET MURDERED POLONIUS, ORDERS A BOAT TO BE PREPARED TO TAKE HAMLET, ROSENCRANTZ AND GUILDENSTERN TO ENGLAND THAT SAME NIGHT WITH A SEALED MESSAGE. AFTER ALL HAVE LEFT, KING CLAUDIUS REVEALS HIS TRUE INTENT...
ENGLAND, IF MY LOVE THOU HOLD'ST AT AUGHT, THOU MAYST NOT COLDLY SET OUR SOVEREIGN PROCESS, WHICH IMPORTS AT FULL, THE PRESENT DEATH OF HAMLET. DO IT, ENGLAND!

THE SHOCK OF HER FATHER'S MYSTERIOUS DEATH, THE MADNESS OF HER LOVER, HAMLET, AND THE LONG ABSENCE OF HER BROTHER, LAERTES, COMBINE TO DRIVE OPHELIA INSANE...
HOW SHOULD I YOUR TRUE LOVE KNOW FROM ANOTHER ONE? BY HIS COCKLE HAT AND STAFF, AND HIS SANDAL SHOON.
TOMORROW IS ST. VALENTINE'S DAY, ALL IN THE MORNING BETIME, AND I A MAID AT YOUR WINDOW, TO BE YOUR VALENTINE.
WHEN SORROWS COME, THEY COME IN BATTALIONS! FIRST, HER FATHER SLAIN; NEXT, YOUR SON GONE; THE PEOPLE MUDDIED THICK AND UNWHOLESOME IN THEIR THOUGHTS OF POLONIUS' DEATH; POOR OPHELIA DIVIDED FROM HERSELF AND HER FAIR JUDGEMENT. LAST, HER BROTHER, IN SECRET COME FROM FRANCE, FEEDS ON HIS WONDER OF HIS FATHER'S DEATH.
A MOMENT LATER, LAERTES STORMS THE CASTLE AT THE HEAD OF A RIOTOUS MOB...
SIRS, STAND YOU ALL WITHOUT. I PRAY YOU, GIVE ME LEAVE.
LAERTES SHALL BE KING! LAERTES KING!
LAERTES CONFRONTS KING CLAUDIUS...
O THOU VILE KING, WHERE IS MY FATHER?

DEAD.
BUT NOT BY HIM.
HOW CAME HE DEAD? I'LL NOT BE JUGGLED WITH; I'LL BE REVENG'D MOST THROUGHLY* FOR MY FATHER.
*THOROUGHLY
IF YOU DESIRE TO KNOW THE CERTAINTY OF YOUR FATHER'S DEATH, IS IT WRIT IN YOUR REVENGE THAT, SWOOPSTAKE*, YOU WILL DRAW BOTH FRIEND AND FOE?
NONE BUT HIS ENEMIES.
*INDISCRIMINATELY
NOW YOU SPEAK LIKE A TRUE GENTLEMAN. THAT I AM GUILTLESS OF YOUR FATHER'S DEATH, AND IN GRIEF FOR IT, YOUR JUDGEMENT SHALL PIERCE.
JUST THEN, OPHELIA WANDERS UPON THE SCENE, AND HER SAD APPEARANCE QUIETS LAERTES...
DO YOU SEE THIS, O GOD?
THEY BORE HIM BAREFAC'D ON THE BIER; HEY, NON, NONNY, NONNY, HEY NONNY; AND IN HIS GRAVE RAIN'D MANY A TEAR.

LAERTES, I MUST COMMUNE WITH YOUR GRIEF. MAKE CHOICE OF YOUR WISEST FRIENDS, AND THEY SHALL HEAR AND JUDGE: IF BY DIRECT OR COLLATERAL HAND THEY FIND US TOUCH'D WE WILL OUR KINGDOM GIVE, OUR CROWN, OUR LIFE, TO YOU IN SATISFACTION; BUT IF NOT, BE CONTENT TO LEND PATIENCE TO US AND WE SHALL JOINTLY LABOUR WITH YOUR SOUL TO GIVE IT DUE CONTENT.
LET THIS BE SO.
HIS MEANS OF DEATH, HIS OBSCURE FUNERAL, NO TROPHY, SWORD, OR HATCHMENT* O'ER HIS BONES, CRY TO BE HEARD, AS 'T WERE FROM HEAVEN TO EARTH, THAT I MUST CALL 'T IN QUESTION.
SO YOU SHALL; AND WHERE THE OFFENCE IS, LET THE GREAT AXE FALL.
*TABLET BEARING THE COAT OF ARMS OF THE DEAD
LATER, HORATIO RECEIVES A LETTER...
THERE'S A LETTER FOR YOU, SIR, IF YOUR NAME BE HORATIO.

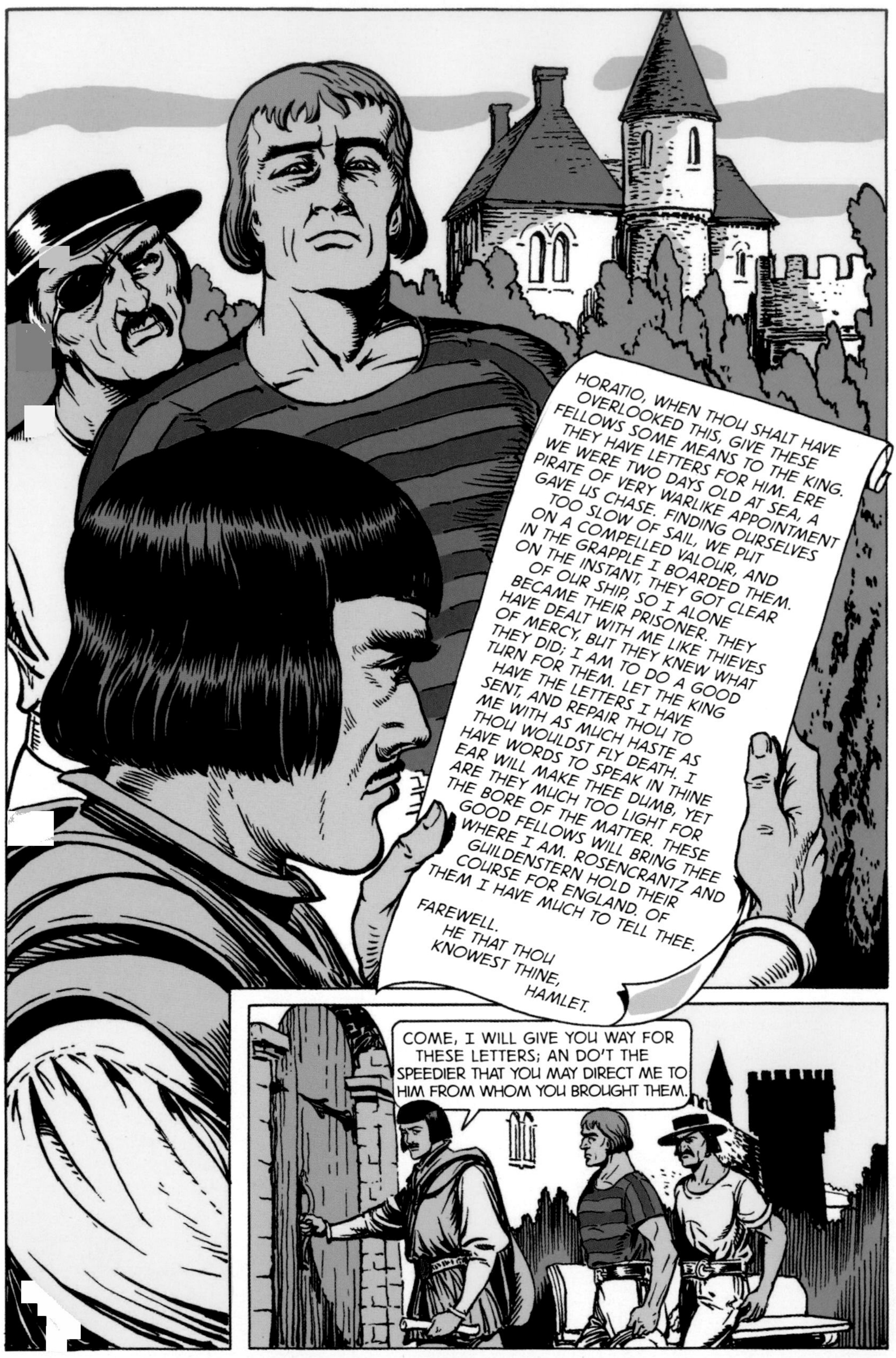
HORATIO, WHEN THOU SHALT HAVE OVERLOOKED THIS, GIVE THESE FELLOWS SOME MEANS TO THE KING. THEY HAVE LETTERS FOR HIM. ERE WE WERE TWO DAYS OLD AT SEA, A PIRATE OF VERY WARLIKE APPOINTMENT GAVE US CHASE. FINDING OURSELVES TOO SLOW OF SAIL, WE PUT ON A COMPELLED VALOUR, AND IN THE GRAPPLE I BOARDED THEM. ON THE INSTANT, THEY GOT CLEAR OF OUR SHIP, SO I ALONE BECAME THEIR PRISONER. THEY HAVE DEALT WITH ME LIKE THIEVES OF MERCY, BUT THEY KNEW WHAT THEY DID; I AM TO DO A GOOD TURN FOR THEM. LET THE KING HAVE THE LETTERS I HAVE SENT, AND REPAIR THOU TO ME WITH AS MUCH HASTE AS THOU WOULDST FLY DEATH. I HAVE WORDS TO SPEAK IN THINE EAR WILL MAKE THEE DUMB, YET ARE THEY MUCH TOO LIGHT FOR THE BORE OF THE MATTER. THESE GOOD FELLOWS WILL BRING THEE WHERE I AM. ROSENCRANTZ AND GUILDENSTERN HOLD THEIR COURSE FOR ENGLAND. OF THEM I HAVE MUCH TO TELL THEE.
FAREWELL.
HE THAT THOU KNOWEST THINE,
HAMLET.
COME, I WILL GIVE YOU WAY FOR THESE LETTERS; AN DO'T THE SPEEDIER THAT YOU MAY DIRECT ME TO HIM FROM WHOM YOU BROUGHT THEM.

MEANWHILE, THE KING HAS TOLD LAERTES HOW HAMLET KILLED HIS FATHER...
AND YOU MUST PUT ME IN YOUR HEART FOR FRIEND. YOU HAVE HEARD THAT HE WHICH HATH YOUR NOBLE FATHER SLAIN PURSUED MY LIFE.
IT WELL APPEARS; BUT TELL ME WHY YOU PROCEEDED NOT AGAINST THESE FEATS, SO CRIMINAL IN NATURE?
FOR TWO SPECIAL REASONS. THE QUEEN LIVES ALMOST BY HIS LOOKS; THE OTHER MOTIVE WHY TO A PUBLIC COUNT I MIGHT NOT GO, IS THE GREAT LOVE THE GENERAL GENDER BEAR HIM.
AND SO HAVE I A NOBLE FATHER LOST, A SISTER DRIVEN INTO DESPERATE TERMS. BUT MY REVENGE WILL COME.
THE COWARDLY KING, THINKING THAT HAMLET IS DEAD IN ENGLAND, SPEAKS BOLD WORDS...
YOU MUST NOT THINK THAT WE ARE MADE OF STUFF SO FLAT AND DULL THAT WE CAN LET OUR BEARD BE SHOOK WITH DANGER AND THINK IT PASTIME. YOU SHORTLY SHALL HEAR MORE.

THE SAILORS GIVE HAMLET'S LETTERS TO A COURT MESSENGER WHO IN TURN DELIVERS IT TO THE KING. THE KING READS THE LETTER ALOUD TO LAERTES...
"HIGH AND MIGHTY, YOU SHALL KNOW I AM SET ON YOUR KINGDOM. TO-MORROW SHALL I BEG LEAVE TO SEE YOUR KINGLY EYES: WHEN I SHALL, FIRST ASKING YOUR PARDON THEREUNTO, RECOUNT THE OCCASION OF MY SUDDEN AND MORE STRANGE RETURN.T HAMLET"
ALARMED, THE KING QUICKLY PLANS ANOTHER WAY TO DESTROY HAMLET...
I WILL WORK HIM TO AN EXPLOIT, NOW RIPE IN MY DEVICE, UNDER WHICH HE SHALL FALL; AND FOR HIS DEATH NO WIND OF BLAME SHALL BREATHE, BUT EVEN HIS MOTHER SHALL CALL IT ACCIDENT. WILL YOU BE RULED BY ME?
MY LORD, I WILL BE RULED, IF YOU COULD DEVISE IT SO THAT I MIGHT BE THE ORGAN.
THE KING UNFOLDS HIS PLAN TO LAERTES. HE BEGINS BY TELLING LAERTES THAT A FRENCH SPORTSMAN, LAMOUND, HAD, A SHORT TIME BEFORE, COME TO DENMARK AND BEFRIENDED HAMLET...

LAMOUND HAD TOLD HAMLET THAT LAERTES WAS CONSIDERED THE BEST SWORDSMAN IN FRANCE AND HAMLET HAD BECOME JEALOUS OF LAERTES' REPUTATION...
I WISH AND BEG LAERTES' SUDDEN COMING O'ER TO PLAY WITH HIM.
AND NOW, HAMLET, HEARING OF LAERTES' RETURN, WILL BE GOADED INTO A MATCH, BY HAVING THE KING'S MEN CONSTANTLY PRAISE LAERTES' ABILITY...
MY LORD, LAERTES IS A VERY FINE SWORDSMAN.
UNDOUBTEDLY THE BEST IN ALL DEMARK.
LAERTES WILL BE ABLE, BY PREARRANGED TREACHERY, TO SELECT AN UNCOVERED FOIL, WHILE HAMLET'S WILL BE BLUNTED...
AND THUS THE UNSUSPECTING HAMLET CAN EASILY BE MURDERED...

LAERTES IS DELIGHTED WITH THE KING'S WICKED SCHEME. HE EVEN OFFERS HIS OWN IMPROVEMENT...
I WILL DO'T. AND, FOR THAT PURPOSE I'LL ANOINT MY SWORD. I BOUGHT AN UNCTION* OF A MOUNTEBANK** SO MORTAL THAT NO CATAPLASM*** CAN SAVE THE THING FROM DEATH THAT IS BUT SCRATCH'D WITHAL. I'LL TOUCH MY POINT WITH THIS CONTAGION.
*POISON **SIDE SHOW MEDICINE MAN ***POULTICE OR ANTIDOTE
AND THEN, IF THESE PLANS ALL FAIL, THE KING HAS HIS OWN POISON, WHICH HE WILL PUT INTO THE GLASS OF WINE THAT HAMLET WILL DRINK DURING THE REST PERIOD OF THE MATCH...
THE QUEEN INTERRUPTS THE PLOTTERS WITH SAD NEWS...
ONE WOE DOTH TREAD UPON ANOTHER'S HEEL, SO FAST THEY FOLLOW: YOUR SISTER'S DROWN'D, LAERTES.
DROWN'D! O, WHERE?

"THERE IS A WILLOW GROWS ASLANT A BROOK THAT SHOWS HIS LEAVES IN THE GLASSY STREAM...
"THERE WITH FANTASTIC GARLANDS DID SHE COME OF CROW-FLOWERS, NETTLES, DAISIES, AND LONG PURPLES...
"THERE, ON THE PENDANT BOUGHS HER CRONET* WEEDS CLAMB'RING TO HANG...
*CORONET
"A SLIVER BROKE: WHEN DOWN HER WEEDY TROPHIES AND HERSELF FELL IN THE WEEPING BROOK...
"HER CLOTHES SPREAD WIDE, A WHILE THEY BORE HER UP, WHICH TIME SHE CHANTED OLD LAUDS*...
*PSALMS OF PRAISE
"TILL HER GARMENTS, HEAVY WITH DRINK, PULL'D THE POOR WRETCH TO MUDDY DEATH..."

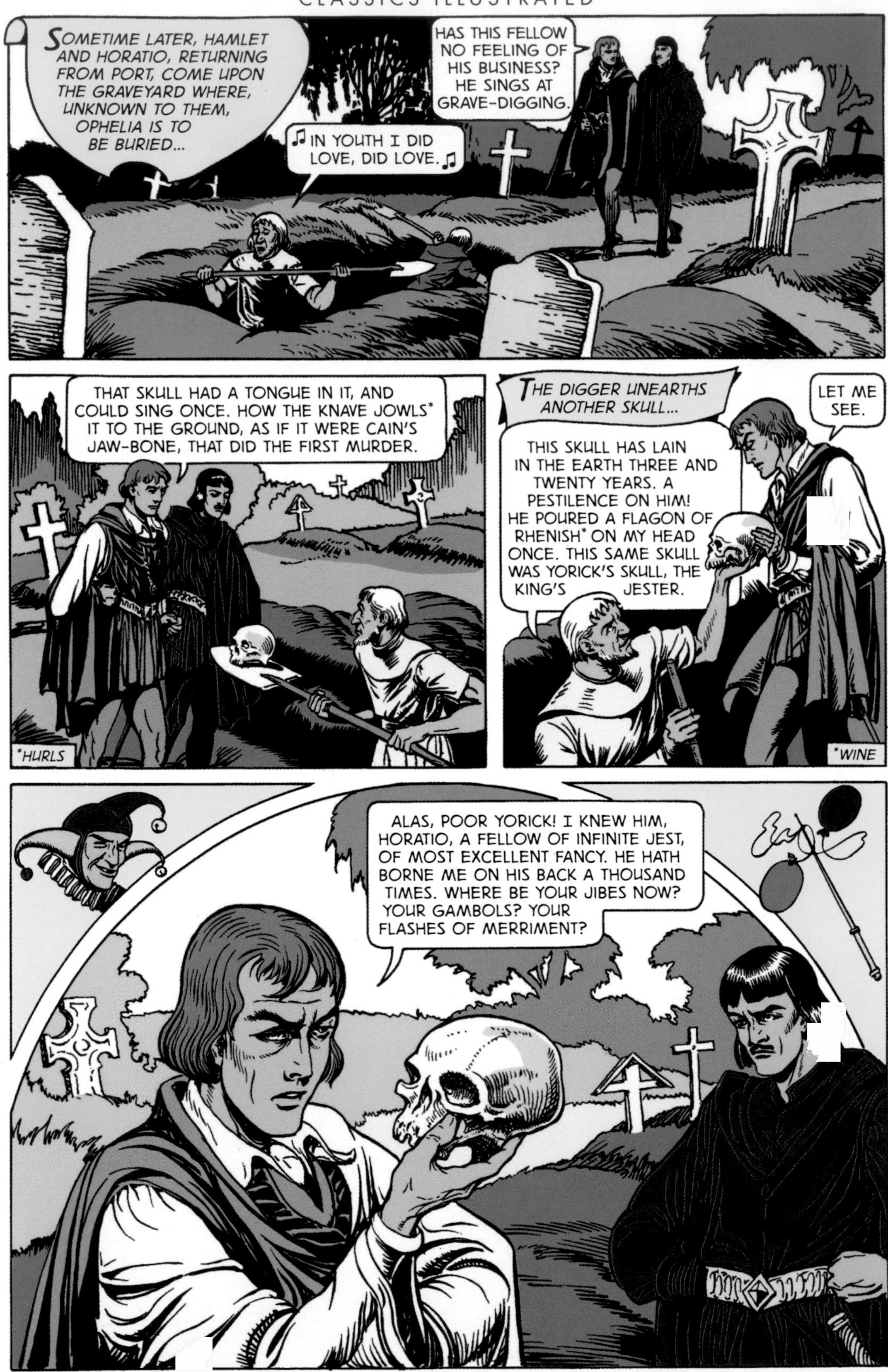
SOMETIME LATER, HAMLET AND HORATIO, RETURNING FROM PORT, COME UPON THE GRAVEYARD WHERE, UNKNOWN TO THEM, OPHELIA IS TO BE BURIED...
♫ IN YOUTH I DID LOVE, DID LOVE. ♫
HAS THIS FELLOW NO FEELING OF HIS BUSINESS? HE SINGS AT GRAVE-DIGGING.
THAT SKULL HAD A TONGUE IN IT, AND COULD SING ONCE. HOW THE KNAVE JOWLS* IT TO THE GROUND, AS IF IT WERE CAIN'S JAW-BONE, THAT DID THE FIRST MURDER.
*HURLS
THE DIGGER UNEARTHS ANOTHER SKULL...
LET ME SEE.
THIS SKULL HAS LAIN IN THE EARTH THREE AND TWENTY YEARS. A PESTILENCE ON HIM! HE POURED A FLAGON OF RHENISH* ON MY HEAD ONCE. THIS SAME SKULL WAS YORICK'S SKULL, THE KING'S JESTER.
*WINE
ALAS, POOR YORICK! I KNEW HIM, HORATIO, A FELLOW OF INFINITE JEST, OF MOST EXCELLENT FANCY. HE HATH BORNE ME ON HIS BACK A THOUSAND TIMES. WHERE BE YOUR JIBES NOW? YOUR GAMBOLS? YOUR FLASHES OF MERRIMENT?

JUST THEN, THE FUNERAL PROCESSION APPROACHES THE GRAVE. HAMLET AND HORATIO, NOT KNOWING WHO IS TO BE BURIED, DO NOT WISH TO INTRUDE ON THE MOURNERS' PRIVACY AND HIDE THEMSELVES...
THE QUEEN, THE COURTIERS. WHO IS THIS THEY FOLLOW? AND WITH SUCH MAIMED RITES? THIS DOTH BETOKEN THE CORSE DID FORDO ITS OWN LIFE. COUCH* WE A WHILE, AND MARK.
*HIDE
WHAT CEREMONY ELSE?
THAT'S LAERTES, A VERY NOBLE YOUTH.

HER OBSEQUIES HAVE BEEN AS FAR ENLARG'D AS WE HAVE WARRANTY. HER DEATH WAS DOUBTFUL; YET HERE SHE IS ALLOWED THE BRINGING HOME OF BELL AND BURIAL
MUST THERE NO MORE BE DONE?
NO MORE. WE SHOULD PROFANE THE SERVICE OF THE DEAD TO SING A REQUIEM AND SUCH REST TO HER AS TO PEACE-PARTED SOULS.
LAY HER IN THE EARTH, AND FROM HER FAIR FLESH MAY VIOLETS SPRING! A MINIST'RING ANGEL SHALL MY SISTER BE.

AS LAERTES USES THE WORD "SISTER", HAMLET RUSHES FORTH...
WHAT, THE FAIR OPHELIA!?
SWEETS TO THE SWEET. I HOP'D THOU SHOULDST HAVE BEEN MY HAMLET'S WIFE.
O, TREBLE WOE FALL ON THAT CURSED HEAD WHOSE WICKED DEED THY SENSE DEPRIV'D THEE OF.

UNABLE TO CONTROL HIS GRIEF, LAERTES LEAPS INTO THE GRAVE...
HOLD OFF THE EARTH A WHILE, TILL I HAVE CAUGHT HER ONCE MORE IN MINE ARMS.
ONLY TO BE FOLLOWED BY HAMLET...
WHAT IS HE WHOSE GRIEF BEARS SUCH AN EMPHASIS? THIS IS I, HAMLET, THE DANE!
PLUCK THEM ASUNDER!
THE DEVIL TAKE THY SOUL!
TAKE THY FINGERS FROM MY THROAT! HOLD OFF THY HAND!

I WILL FIGHT WITH HIM! I LOV'D OPHELIA! FORTY THOUSAND BROTHERS COLD NOT, WITH ALL THEIR LOVE, MAKE UP MY SUM.
FOR LOVE OF GOD, FORBEAR HIM.
LAERTES, STRENGTHEN YOUR PATIENCE IN OUR LAST NIGHT'S SPEECH. WE'LL PUT THE MATTER TO THE PUSH.
BACK IN THE CASTLE, HAMLET TELLS HORATIO THAT ON HIS TRIP TO ENGLAND, HE HAD STOLEN AND BROKEN OPEN THE SEALED LETTER ROSENCRANTZ WAS CARRYING...
AH, ROYAL KNAVERY! I FOUND A COMMAND THAT, ON THE SUPERVISE, NO LEISURE BATED, NO, NOT TO STAY THE GRINDING OF THE AXE, MY HEAD SHOULD BE STRUCK OFF.
HAMLET THEN TELLS HORATIO THAT HE WROTE ANOTHER LETTER ORDERING THAT THE BEARERS BE PUT DEATH... AND PLACED IT IN ROSENCRANTZ'S BAG. AT THE SAME TIME, HE DESTROYED THE ORDER FOR HIS OWN EXECUTION...
I HAD MY FATHER'S SIGNET IN MY PURSE, WHICH WAS THE MODEL FOR THE DANISH SEAL; FOLDED THE WRIT UP IN THE FORM OF THE OTHER, SUBSCRIB'D IT, GAVE'T THE IMPRESSION, PLAC'D IT SAFELY. THE NEXT DAY WAS OUR SEA FIGHT; WHAT WAS SEQUENT THOU KNOWEST.
SO GUILDENSTERN AND ROSENCRANTZ GO TO'T.
THEY ARE NOT NEAR MY CONSCIENCE; THEIR DEFEAT DOES BY THEIR OWN INSINUATION GROW.

A MESSENGER BRINGS WORD THAT THE KING WISHES HAMLET TO MEET LAERTES IN A FRIENDLY DUEL, THUS DISPERSING THE AIR OF ENMITY BETWEEN THE TWO. HAMLET, SOMEWHAT DISTRESSED BY HIS QUARREL WITH LAERTES, FALLS EASILY INTO THE TRAP SET FOR HIM BY THE EVIL KING AND THE VENGEFUL LAERTES. BEFORE STARTING THE MATCH, HAMLET MAKES FRIENDLY OVERTURES TO HIS OPPONENT...
GIVE ME YOUR PARDON, SIR. I HAVE DONE YOU WRONG, BUT PARDON 'T. WHAT I HAVE DONE, I PROCLAIM WAS MADNESS.
I DO RECEIVE YOUR OFFER'D LOVE LIKE LOVE, AND WILL NOT WRONG IT.
AFTER THIS EXCHANGE, HAMLET AND LAERTES CHOOSE THEIR WEAPONS. HAMLET, OF COURSE, CHOOSES HIS AT RANDOM, WHILST LAERTES PICKS UP THE FOIL WHICH HAS BEEN UNTIPPED AND IMBUED WITH POISON...
TRUMPETS SOUND AND THE "FRIENDLY" MATCH BEGINS. THE FIRST TO SCORE THREE HITS WILL BE DECLARED THE WINNER...
COME ON, SIR.
COME, MY LORD.
AFTER A FEW MOMENTS...
ONE.
NO.
JUDGEMENT.
A HIT, A VERY PALPABLE HIT.
WELL; AGAIN.

THE KING, FEARING THAT HAMLET'S FINE SWORDSMANSHIP MAY SAVE HIM FROM LAERTES' POISONED FOIL, PREPARES A CUP OF POISONED WINE FOR THE YOUNG PRINCE...
STAY, HAMLET, HERE'S TO THY HEALTH. GIVE HIM THE CUP.
I'LL PLAY THIS BOUT FIRST; SET IT BY A WHILE.
COME. ANOTHER HIT; WHAT SAY YOU?
A TOUCH, A TOUCH, I DO CONFESS 'T.
OUR SON SHALL WIN.
HE'S FAT AND SCANT OF BREATH*. HERE, HAMLET, TAKE MY NAPKIN AND RUB THY BROW. THE QUEEN CAROUSES TO THY FORTUNE.
*IN POOR CONDITION
AND THE QUEEN DRINKS THE POISONED WINE THAT HAD BEEN INTENDED FOR HER SON...
GERTRUDE, DO NOT DRINK!
I WILL, MY LORD. I PRAY YOU, PARDON ME.
MY LORD, I'LL HIT HIM NOW.
I DO NOT THINK'T.
AND YET, IT IS ALMOST AGAINST MY CONSCIENCE.
COME, FOR THE THIRD, LAERTES.

AFTER A FEW MOMENTS OF SPARRING, LAERTES FINALLY BREAKS THROUGH HAMLET'S DEFENCE. BUT INSTEAD OF BEING SIMPLY HIT, HAMLET IS ASTOUNDED AND INFURIATED TO FIND THAT HE HAS BEEN WOUNDED BY AN UNTIPPED FOIL. HE NOW REALISES LAERTES' TRUE INTENT AND RUSHES MADLY AT HIS OPPONENT. AS THEY SCUFFLE, THEY BOTH DROP THEIR FOILS. IN THE ENSUING CONFUSION, THEY MISTAKENLY EXCHANGE FOILS...
PART THEM; THEY ARE INCENS'D.
NAY, COME AGAIN.
WITH A LIGHTNING-LIKE STROKE AND THRUST, HAMLET MORTALLY WOUNDS LAERTES. AT THE SAME MOMENT, THE QUEEN FALLS FROM HER CHAIR...
THEY BLEED ON BOTH SIDES. HOW IS'T, MY LORD?
HOW IS'T LAERTES?
WHY, I AM JUSTLY KILLED WITH MINE OWN TREACHERY.
HOW DOES THE QUEEN?
SHE SWOONS TO SEE THEM BLEED.
NO, NO, THE DRINK, THE DRINK – O MY DEAR HAMLET, THE DRINK, THE DRINK! I AM POISONED!

NOW THAT YOU HAVE READ THE CLASSICS ILLUSTRATED EDITION, WHY NOT GO ON TO READ THE ORIGINAL VERSION TO GET THE FULL ENJOYMENT OF THIS CLASSIC WORK?

Murder, revenge, sex, politics, and a ghost - with ingredients like these, it's no wonder that *Hamlet* is one of the most famous of William Shakespeare's plays, and one of the most often performed. Some of Shakespeare's plays have gone in and out of fashion since his death (*A Midsummer Night's Dream* didn't appeal to audiences of the 19th Century, for example, and women in a late 20th Century audience are not likely to find *The Taming of the Shrew* as amusing as they might have in earlier times), but *Hamlet* has been with us steadily since the beginning.

Historical Content

Hamlet was written and first performed during the period when England was moving from the Elizabethan era to the Jacobean. Elizabeth Tudor died in 1603, and James VI of Scotland came to the throne of England as James I. James was a Scot, the son of Elizabeth Tudor's cousin Mary, and he was nowhere near as charismatic and popular as his predecessor, Elizabeth, had been.

Elizabeth had ruled England for forty-five years, and had become almost a secular idol in the minds of her subjects. She wasn't just Elizabeth Tudor. She was Gloriana, the Virgin Queen, who said of herself, "I may have the body of a weak and feeble woman, but I have the heart and stomach of a King, and a King of England, too," and who said to her people, "Though you have had, and may have, many wiser princes sitting in this seat, yet you never had, nor shall have, any that will love you better." The European rulers who were her contemporaries saw Elizabeth in a different but equally formidable aspect. Henry of Navarre, later King Henry IV of France, said of her admiringly, "She only is a king. She only knows how to rule!"

Elizabeth Tudor, in short, was going to be a hard act to follow, and James Stuart didn't look like he was the person to do it. He was a clumsy, unhandsome man, pathologically afraid of assassination - he wore thickly padded doublets to protect himself against knife attacks - and of attack by witchcraft. He was also vehemently opposed to the new habit of smoking, calling it foul and unhealthful. (He was dead right on that one, as it happens, but he didn't get any credit for it at the time, and smokers kept on polluting the air for almost four centuries before anybody raised the subject again.)

James the First was no Gloriana; he had, instead, the dubious honour of being known as "the wisest fool in Christendom."

Hamlet's Soliloquies

If Hamlet isn't crazy (or at least, isn't crazy all of the time), then why does he talk to himself so much? The answer lies in the conventions - the accepted ways for showing things - of the Elizabethan stage. Actors could indicate a change of time or place for the audience by talking about it, and have the description accepted as part of the dialogue, even though people in everyday conversation seldom bother to describe their surroundings to each other. Likewise, the audience would accept that a character might speak to them directly, either in brief comments (known as "asides") made during conversations with other characters, or in longer speeches made while the character was alone on the stage ("soliloquies").

Cont'd

A character's asides are "heard" only by the audience, even though other characters may be on the stage at the time. Soliloquies, also, are heard in this fashion - some of them were in fact addressed to the audience directly. The invisible wall between the characters and the audience was not then as high and thick as it later became. Another convention of the aside and the soliloquy is that the character who's speaking is telling the truth, and that his or her words can be trusted to a higher degree than words spoken between characters.

In none of Shakespeare's plays are soliloquies more important than in *Hamlet*. One of Hamlet's main problems is determining how and what he should think about a particular thing, the death of his father. The use of the soliloquy technique allows Shakespeare to give the audience a glimpse of Hamlet thinking, and lets him make the process of thought into something dramatically interesting. Also, the soliloquies emphasise Hamlet's lonely and isolated role at the court of Denmark. He must keep a close watch over his tongue, and not say anything he doesn't intend to say (and in fact, most of what Hamlet does say in public has multiple meanings - sharp, rather nasty jokes and puns). When he's alone, therefore, it's not surprising that his speech becomes wild and overwrought in reaction to the sudden freedom.

The Problem of the Ghost

What is the real nature of the ghost? Is it in fact the spirit of the dead king, or is it some kind of supernatural (and probably demonic) being? And is it even telling the truth?

It's difficult for modern audiences to appreciate just how serious a problem the ghost and its call to vengeance pose for Hamlet. Since we don't (most of us) believe either in ghosts or in the need for private justice, our tendency is to accept the ghost at face value as a plot device, and therefore spend the rest of the play wondering why Hamlet doesn't just get on with the revenge business.

Shakespeare's audience, however, believed both in ghosts and demons. Likewise, revenge - while certainly not a part of everybody's daily life - was still an open matter for debate. From Hamlet's point of view, the ghost is a real thing, no question; the difficulty lies in determining what kind of a real thing. (Note that the ghost is seen first by the soldiers on the wall, and later by the solidly normal and rational Horatio, before Hamlet ever lays eyes on it.) The very first time Hamlet addresses the ghost, he makes his doubts and worries plain:

> *"Be thou a spirit of health or goblin damned,*
> *Bring with thee airs from heaven or blasts from hell,*
> *Be thy intents wicked or charitable,*
> *Thou com'st in such a questionable shape*
> *That I will speak to thee."*

Cont'd

This is, in fact, the whole difficulty in a nutshell. The spectre on the battlements of Elsinore may indeed be Hamlet's father's ghost, telling a true story and calling on his son to do his duty as heir to the throne. If the ghost is real and speaks truth, then an act of murder is going unpunished, and Hamlet, as a member of the royal family, is perhaps the only person at court highly placed enough to carry out justice. If the ghost's story is true, the current ruler of the kingdom has no real right to the throne - a state of affairs which, given the almost mystical identity believed to exist between monarch and kingdom, could have serious consequences for everyone in Denmark.

Neither Hamlet nor Shakespeare's audience, however, could afford to forget the other possibility: that the apparition which appeared on the castle battlements was not a true ghost, but a demon from Hell taking on a ghostly form in order to tempt the Prince of Denmark into the sin of murder. Hamlet sums up the problem, for himself and the audience, when he decides to use the visiting troupe of actors to set up a test of the king's guilt:

"...The spirit that I have seen
May be a devil, and the devil hath power
T'assume a pleasing shape; yea, and perhaps,
Out of my weakness and my melancholy,
As he is very potent with such spirits,
Abuses me to damn me. I'll have grounds
More relative than this. The play's the thing
Wherein I'll catch the conscience of the King."

Later, just before the performance, he tells Horatio the same thing:

"Observe my uncle. If his occulted [hidden] guilt
Do not itself unkennel in one speech,
It is a damned ghost that we have seen,
And my imaginations are as foul
As Vulcan's stithy [forge]."

If we go by the beliefs of the day, several things argue in favour of the demonic theory: The ghost is visibly offended when Horatio orders it to speak "by Heaven"; it vanishes when the cock crows; it is an angry spirit, and comes to Hamlet armed and armoured; and it speaks from beneath the ground, the traditional abode of demons and evil spirits. Most importantly, the ghost urges Hamlet toward committing a deed which would at worst be murder and regicide, and which even at best would involve taking on a task which rightfully belongs to God alone.

Given these conflicting possibilities, and given how much is at stake (nothing less than the health of the state of Denmark and of his own immortal soul) Hamlet is impelled to look for outside confirmation of the ghost's accusations. Hence the "Mousetrap", the play-within-the-play depicting the murder of a king by his brother, which Hamlet uses as a sort of psychological test.

Revenge, Regicide and Usurpation

Why doesn't Hamlet act promptly to avenge his father, as Fortinbras does, and as Laertes does when he hears of the death of Polonius?

Cont'd

At the time Shakespeare was writing *Hamlet* (and re-writing *Hamlet*; there seem to have been at least three different versions put on by the Lord Chamberlain's Men between 1599 and 1603, with no way for us to determine which one was the author's "preferred cut") revenge was a popular literary device. Most people, however, accepted the idea that seeking revenge was a sin; vengeance belonged to God and justice belonged to the State. Private justice might have been necessary in "the old days," or in barbarous countries like Scotland or Italy or Spain, but proper Englishmen had lawyers and judges to settle their problems for them. Revenge - intended, planned and carried out - was a killing in cold blood, and unlikely to gain the complete sympathy of an English audience no matter how much it entertained them.

Furthermore, even if the ghost is what it seems to be, and is speaking truth, Hamlet still faces no light problem. Claudius may be the murderer of Hamlet's father, but he is also the King of Denmark and not just any common or garden variety villain. The problem of regicide (literally, "king-killing") was a hot topic in Shakespeare's day. In a period when monarchs ruled for life, and ruled absolutely, killing the king was often the only way to bring about changes at the top. At the same time, kings were not, in the mind of the day, ordinary men. When Claudius tells Gertrude, "There's such divinity doth hedge a king," he means it - the king is not God, but is God-like in a worldly sense, and stands in relation to the kingdom as God does to the universe as a whole.

Killing a king, or killing a ruling queen, was not just murder but a kind of sacrilege, a religious as well as a civil crime. Not that this had ever stopped people from trying: Elizabeth I had often been the target of assassination plots, as had James I - whose father, Henry Lord Darnley, had been killed by Earl Bothwell, and whose mother, Mary Queen of Scots, was herself imprisoned and, ultimately, executed by order of her cousin Elizabeth.

Closely related to the problem of regicide was the problem of usurpation - the stealing of the kingship from the rightful heir by another claimant. English history gives us a number of instances of such royal theft. Henry VII, the founder of the Tudor dynasty, took over the throne after defeating Richard III at the Battle of Bosworth Field; and Richard III may or may not have come to the throne illicitly himself, after first declaring the two sons of his brother Edward IV illegitimate, and then having them murdered.

A number of Shakespeare's plays deal with themes of regicide and usurpation - *Richard II*, *Julius Caesar* and *Macbeth*, to name only three of them - and other plays such as *The Tempest*, *King Lear* and *As You like It* feature deposed or dispossessed dukes and princes. Getting rid of a bad or incompetent king, by whatever means, was a matter for intense intellectual debate all through the 16th and 17th centuries. Eventually, debate changed to action. In 1649, James's son, Charles I, would be executed by the English Parliament at the end of a nasty civil war, and the "divinity [that] doth hedge a king" would never be the same again.

Discussion Topics

1) The ghost of Hamlet's father is seen by Marcellus, Bernardo and Horatio at the beginning of the play, and also at the time of its first appearance to Hamlet. However, when the ghost appears again during the confrontation with Gertrude after the play-within-a-play, Hamlet sees it but Gertrude does not. What do you think may be the reason or reasons for this change?

2) What might have happened if Hamlet had decided to ignore the ghost's commands? Would Claudius eventually have repented? What other effects might have come about because of the crime hidden at the heart of Denmark's royal family?

3) Fortinbras, when he arrives at the Danish court just in time to view the carnage, says of Hamlet, "he was likely, had he been put on [made king] to have proved most royal." In your opinion, is this a fair judgement? Which of Hamlet's qualities might have worked to make him a good king, and which might have made him a bad or an ineffectual one? Who might have been a better king of Denmark in the long run, Hamlet or Claudius, and why?

4) Look at all the references in *Hamlet* to weeds, and then at the references to flowers, gardening and agriculture. Which characters make such references, and in what circumstances? Is there a pattern to the references? Do you think this pattern has anything to do with why Ophelia uses flower-symbolism in her madness ("There's rosemary, that's for remembrance"), and why she meets her death while picking fresh flowers? Why or why not?

Timeline

1588 - The Spanish Armada is defeated by an English naval force under the command of Lord Charles Howard and Sir Francis Drake.

1592 - Trinity College, Dublin, Ireland's oldest university, is founded.

1595 - Shakespeare's play *Romeo and Juliet* is first performed.

1596 - Sir Francis Drake, English explorer and soldier, dies.

1598 - Boris Godunov seizes the throne of Russia, following the death of his brother-in-law, Tsar Feodor I; the Time of Troubles starts.

The Parliament of England passes an act that allows transportation of convicts to colonies.

1599 - The Globe Theatre is opened in London.

1599-1602 - William Shakespeare writes *Hamlet* under its full name, *The Tragedy of Hamlet, Prince of Denmark*.

1603 - Elizabeth I of England dies and is succeeded by her cousin's grandson, King James VI of Scotland, uniting the crowns of Scotland and England.

1605 - Gunpowder Plot: A conspiracy to blow up the English Houses of Parliament is foiled when Sir Thomas Knyvet, a justice of the peace, finds Guy Fawkes in a cellar below the Parliament building and orders a search of the area where 36 barrels of gunpowder are found.

1606 - Guy Fawkes is executed.